THIS BOOK BELONGS TO

Happy Birthday

Jon
Wallace
Wells

Published by Longmeadow Press, 201 High Ridge Road, Stamford, Connecticut 06904. ISBN 0-681-40326-8. Printed in the U.S.A. 0 9 8 7 6 5 4 3 2 1

Happy Birthday, Walter!
A Counting Book

**By Don Ross
and
Sue Levytsky
Illustrated by Don Ross**

Longmeadow Press

"Happy Birthday, dear Walter.
Happy Birthday to you.
Count your birthday as special.
A day just for you!
What would you like to do?"

"I know!"
said Walter.

The first thing I'll do
On my special day
Is climb into ONE shoe
And sail far, far away.

I'll sail that shoe
Someplace thrilling and new.
And when I'm there,
Do you know what I'll do?

I'll meet my friend Dennis.
We'll have a chase.
Around Moose Mountain,
We'll race, race, race.

Count me, count Dennis,
Count one and TWO.
We'll race to the finish.
Then what will I do?

I'll enter a contest
To ride pogo-roos.
Jump over the clouds.
Yes, that's what I'll do!

Count one and two.
Count one, two, THREE.
What will I do next?
Come along and you'll see.

I'll go to the park and
Play golf with my friends.
We'll play four holes
Before the course ends.

Count one, count two,
Count three and FOUR.
Now we'll do something
I'll like even more.

We'll float through the clouds
and soar through the sky.

My four friends and I
Will fly so high.

We're ready to land.
Where will we arrive?

Count all the balloons.
Count one through FIVE.

Deep in the jungle
It's scary, it's hot.
We're on an adventure
Which we like a lot.

Count SIX, five, four,
Three, two and one.
What happens next?
It's on to more fun.

We'll climb Candy Mountain
In a clackety train.
Eat chocolates for lunch and
Drink orange juice rain.

From one to SEVEN
Count the whole row.
That was delicious.
Now where shall we go?

From EIGHT to one,
Count back up to eight.
What we do next
Should really be great.

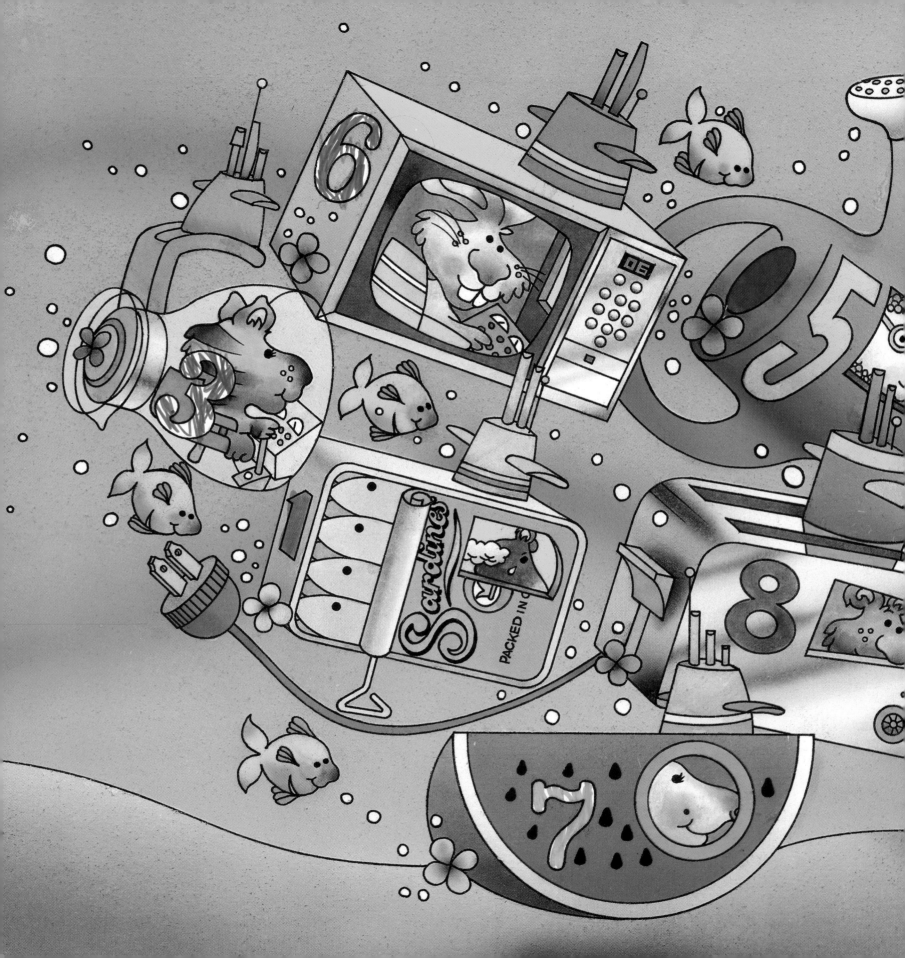

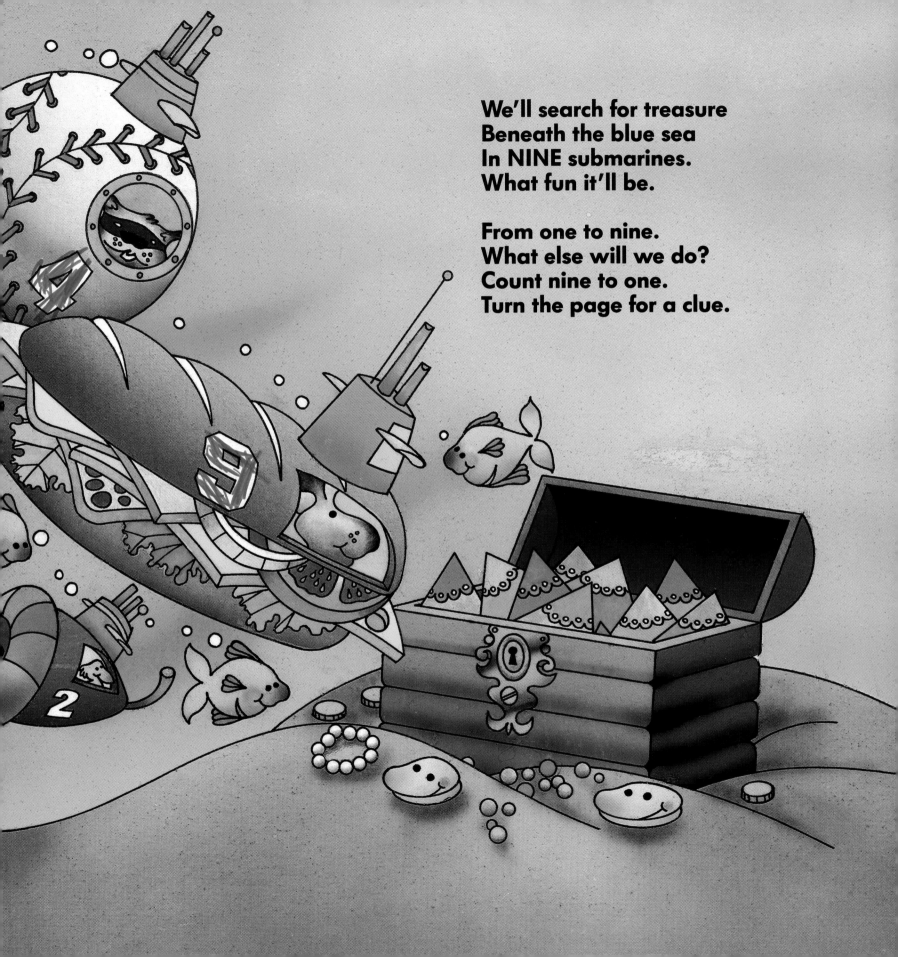

We'll search for treasure
Beneath the blue sea
In NINE submarines.
What fun it'll be.

From one to nine.
What else will we do?
Count nine to one.
Turn the page for a clue.

Since a birthday party
Is part of Mom's plan,
We'll all run home
As fast as we can.

here'll be ice cream and punch
nd lots of cake.

I'll blow out the candles.
Here's the wish that I'll make.

I hope that I'll always have
Friends just like you
To count on my birthday
And other days, too.

Count all of my friends.
From TEN to one.
Sharing with friends
Made this birthday fun.